J   Hurwitz, Johanna.
           Aldo Peanut Butter.

$12.95   *WITHDRAWN*

JUL 1 1 1991	DATE		

By Johanna Hurwitz

The Adventures of Ali Baba Bernstein
Aldo Applesauce
Aldo Ice Cream
Baseball Fever
Busybody Nora
Class Clown
Class President
The Cold and Hot Winter
DeDe Takes Charge!
The Hot and Cold Summer
Hurray for Ali Baba Bernstein
Hurricane Elaine
The Law of Gravity
Much Ado About Aldo
New Neighbors for Nora
Nora and Mrs. Mind-Your-Own-Business
Once I Was a Plum Tree
The Rabbi's Girls
Rip-Roaring Russell
Russell and Elisa
Russell Rides Again
Russell Sprouts
Superduper Teddy
Teacher's Pet
Tough-Luck Karen
Yellow Blue Jay

ALDO
Peanut Butter

JOHANNA HURWITZ

ILLUSTRATED BY
DIANE de GROAT

MORROW JUNIOR BOOKS
NEW YORK

Printed in the United States of America.
1 2 3 4 5 6 7 8 9 10

Library of Congress Cataloging-in-Publication Data

Hurwitz, Johanna.
Aldo Peanut Butter / Johanna Hurwitz ; illustrated by
Diane de Groat.
p.   cm.
Summary: Peanut and Butter, the two dogs Aldo gets for his
eleventh birthday, create chaos inside the house while his parents
are out of town and get accused of tearing up the neighbor's lawn.
ISBN 0-688-09751-0.
[1. Dogs—Fiction. 2. Family life—Fiction.] I. De Groat,
Diane, ill. II. Title. III. Title: Aldo.
PZ7.H9574Ap 1990
[Fic]—dc20   90-35366   CIP   AC

For two special people,
Shula and Henry Mustacchi

Contents

ALDO Peanut Butter

1

What's in a Name?

On Aldo Sossi's eleventh birthday, he received five dogs. His sister Elaine gave him a dog, and so did his sister Karen. His parents gave him a dog, and so did his best friend, DeDe Rawson. And he gave one to himself. After all, he had reasoned, it was his birthday. He should be able to give himself whatever he wanted on his own special day. Of course, he hadn't known about the four other dogs that he would be receiving. Each one was a surprise.

It was hard to know who was the most surprised by the arrival of five dogs at the Sossi home—Aldo who received them or each of the people who had arranged for him to celebrate his birthday with such a lively gift. Probably the one who was the most surprised was Aldo's mother. Like her son, Mrs. Sossi was fond of animals. But no one could like *five* dogs in one home. Especially not five dogs that were puppies. That meant that none of them was housebroken. And besides, the family already had a cat named Peabody. Something had to be done about the surplus of dogs, and it had to be done fast.

"You'll have to make a choice. One dog is enough for any family," Mr. Sossi said at first.

Still, Aldo's parents didn't want to deprive their son of so many of his birthday presents. If he kept two of the puppies, it wouldn't be as much work as keeping five. And the puppies would be companions for each other when Aldo was away at school.

So in the end, a compromise was reached. Aldo was permitted to keep two of the puppies, and new homes were quickly found for the others.

Aldo chose to keep the puppy that he had brought home for himself. It was the mostly brown, curly-haired daughter of a clever mutt named Einstein.

The other dog he kept was the one his parents had given him. It was also a mixed breed, white in color and short-haired.

"What are you going to name them?" Karen asked her brother.

"I don't know," Aldo said. "I'll have to think about it a bit."

"They should have names that go together," Elaine said. "Something like Tarzan and Jane. Or Romeo and Juliet."

"No good," said Aldo. "They're both females. And I don't like the names Jane and Juliet."

"You could name them Rose and Lilac," suggested Karen. "I love flower names for people. There's an Iris in my class at school and there used to be a Heather."

"Flower names?" said Aldo. "No, thanks. Save that for your kids. Besides, I think flower names belong on flowers."

"I have an idea," suggested Mr. Sossi. "Why don't we all make lists of names? Then Aldo can select an appropriate name from our lists."

So Sunday morning, the day after Aldo's birthday, found all five of the human members of the family sitting with sheets of paper and making lists.

"Just a minute," said Mrs. Sossi, looking up from her list. "Did you walk the puppies? I don't want any accidents on the floor."

"I walked them as soon as I got up," said Aldo. "And I walked them again after I ate my breakfast."

"They look so cute," sighed Karen. Einstein's daughter was sleeping cuddled up inside a carton in the kitchen. The white dog was sitting on Aldo's lap.

"Shh. I can't think when everyone is talking," complained Elaine. She was busy scribbling down names.

Aldo chewed on his pencil, and the white puppy in his lap reached up and began chewing on the collar of Aldo's rugby shirt.

"Here's my list," said Karen. "I didn't put down any flower names. But they're all beautiful." She read them aloud. "Amanda, Samantha, Danielle, Gabrielle, Susannah, Roxanna, Veronica . . ."

"Stop, stop," Aldo protested. "Those are terrible. They're people names. Can you imagine me saying, 'Roxanna made a puddle on the living room floor.' "

"No, I can't imagine it and I don't want to hear it, either," said Mrs. Sossi. "No puddles, and no sugary names, either. How about some down-to-earth *dog* names like Trixie and Pixie or Spot and Rover?"

"Boring," complained Elaine. "Listen to these. I made them into pairs and I think some of them are just super." She began to rattle off the names that she had thought of—Salt and Pepper, Yankee and Doodle, Hocus and Pocus.

Einstein's daughter jumped out of the box where she had been sleeping and began to yelp.

"I don't think she likes those names," said Aldo. "And to tell you the truth, neither do I."

"No, no. Stop!" shouted Mrs. Sossi as Einstein's daughter began to make a small puddle on the kitchen floor.

"Bad dog, bad dog," Mr. Sossi called out as he ran to get some paper towels to take care of the problem.

"I have a feeling that these dogs are going to be called Stop and No. That's all I've been saying to them since they arrived," moaned Mrs. Sossi.

"Stop and No sounds like Stop and Go. That's a good pair," said Elaine.

"It would be perfect for a red dog and a green dog." Karen giggled.

Aldo got up and put the white dog on the floor. Then he picked up Einstein's daughter and spoke to her gently. "Were you telling me that you had to go outside?" he asked. "I'm sorry I didn't understand. I'm just learning dog talk."

"You're going to have to walk these puppies more often," said his mother. "Otherwise, we'll be flooded in here. You better take the other one outside right now before we have another accident."

"Too late," said Karen, looking in the direction of the white dog. The dog was sniffing at a small puddle that hadn't been on the floor a moment ago.

"The paper towel industry never had it so good," said Mr. Sossi as he went to get a few more sheets from the roller.

"I'm taking both dogs outside right now," said Aldo.

"That's like locking the barn after the horse is gone," commented Elaine.

"Thank goodness we haven't got a horse," said Mrs. Sossi.

"You don't have to housebreak horses," Karen pointed out. "They never come inside the house."

"No, but you have to feed them and groom them and goodness knows what else. Don't tell me. I don't want to know. I promise you, we'll never own a horse," her mother said.

Aldo put on his jacket and attached the leashes to the collars of both dogs. "When I grow up, I want to have at least one of everything—a horse, a cow, a chicken, a pig, a goat. . . ."

"How about a wife?" asked Karen.

"He'll never find a wife who wants to live with him *and* a whole zoo," said Elaine.

"He's only eleven. Give him time. Maybe he will," said Karen.

"See you later," Aldo called. He didn't mind being teased about his love for animals. He was planning to be a veterinarian when he grew up. He liked his family, but he sometimes felt he liked animals even more. They didn't tease and they didn't complain. Animals just wanted to be fed and loved and they'd love you back.

Outside, the puppies both pulled at their leashes. Einstein's daughter pulled to the left, and the white pup pulled to the right. Aldo held tight and tried to walk straight ahead. When that seemed impossible, he made a quick decision and walked toward the right. Left would have pulled him out onto the street. "Next time we'll go where you want to," he told the dog who didn't get her way.

"Aldo, wait up," a voice called.

Aldo couldn't wait up. Now both puppies were pulling him toward the right. But he recognized the voice. It was his friend DeDe.

"Hi," she called, slightly out of breath, as she ran toward him. "How's it going?"

"Great!" said Aldo. "They both slept under my bed, and we've only had a few accidents so far. My mother didn't like that, but she'll get used to it."

"No, she won't," said DeDe. "But after a while, they won't have accidents."

"I'm sorry I couldn't keep the dog you gave me," said Aldo. "But he's got a good home, and we can visit him whenever we want."

"That's okay," said DeDe. "He didn't cost any-

■ 8 ■

thing. My neighbor's dog had puppies, and she wanted to get rid of them."

"How's Cookie?" asked Aldo. Cookie was DeDe's dog.

"She's fine. I left her home until your dogs are better trained. I was afraid they'd be scared if she barked at them. She's so much bigger than they are."

DeDe took one of the leashes from Aldo, and the two friends walked together down the street.

"Did you give them names yet?" DeDe asked.

"Everyone in my family is busy working on names for them. It's crazy. After all, they are my dogs. You'd think they'd just leave me alone and let me do it. But, no, everyone wants to get in on the act."

"I don't blame them," said DeDe. "Naming's fun."

"How did you get the idea to name Cookie, Cookie?"

"I don't remember. I think it was one of the three words I knew at the time," said DeDe. "Mama, Dada, and Cookie. Neither of my parents wanted the dog named after them, and so my dog became Cookie."

"It's a nice name," said Aldo. "It has a nice, friendly sound to it."

"That's because you like cookies," said DeDe. "Pick another food."

"That's a funny way to name a dog," said Aldo.

"One dog is white and one is brown. They could be Milk and Cocoa," suggested DeDe. "Or Mashed Potato and Hamburger. That's another possibility."

"I wouldn't have a dog named Hamburger. I'm a vegetarian," Aldo reminded his friend. "I don't eat any meat." Aldo had been a vegetarian ever since he was in third grade and his class had studied the food chain. His mother had thought he would give it up after a little while, but instead, Aldo had just become more and more firm in his resolve not to eat meat. How could he eat animals when he liked them so much?

They walked along naming brown and white combinations of food: coffee and cream, chocolate and vanilla, chocolate and marshmallow, gravy and potatoes. The choices seemed endless.

"You have to think of a name pretty soon," DeDe warned Aldo. "One of the first things you have to do when you train a dog is teach her her name. Then when she is good or bad, you use it. And she learns from your voice how you feel about her behavior. You can't say 'good doggie' if one of them is good, because the other one might be bad and think you're talking to her."

"I hadn't thought of that," Aldo admitted. "Okay, then. I won't go back into the house until I decide on a pair of names. You should hear some of the crazy ones they've come up with at home. Things like Gabrielle and Samantha."

"Yuck," said DeDe.

Einstein's daughter stopped pulling at the leash and made a tiny puddle on the ground. "Good dog, good dog," said Aldo, petting the little brown puppy.

"Quick, give her a name," said DeDe.

"Peanut," said Aldo. "Good Peanut!"

"Peanut she is!" said DeDe. "Good work. Now how about the other one?"

"What goes with Peanut?" asked Aldo helplessly. The first name had just popped into his head. Now he was drawing a blank when he tried to think of a second name.

"Butter?" suggested DeDe.

"Peanut and Butter. Peanut Butter. Elaine would like that. She was trying to make pairs of words that went together."

"This dog isn't really the color of butter," DeDe observed.

"I don't care," said Aldo. "Your dog Cookie sure doesn't look like something anyone would want to bite into. So Butter here doesn't have to resemble butter, either." He bent down and gave the dog a hug. "She's soft like butter when it stays out of the refrigerator for a while," he said, standing up again. "Come on, let's go home. I want to tell my family about the names."

They turned back and went to Aldo's home. As they entered, Aldo called out to everyone. "Peanut and Butter," he shouted.

"It's too close to lunchtime," said Mrs. Sossi. "You can't have anything to eat now. You'll just have to wait a little while."

Aldo laughed. "I don't want to eat. I'm telling you the names of the puppies. They're Peanut and

Butter. Peanut Butter. What do you think of that?"

"It makes me hungry," said Karen, bending down to hug the white pup that had gone outside nameless but was now Butter.

"No fair," called out Mr. Sossi. "You never even gave me a chance to present my names: Mona and Lisa."

"Too late," said Aldo. "Save your names for the next pet we get."

"No more. No more," called out Mrs. Sossi. "Peanut, Butter, and Peabody. That's enough for any family." And in the days that followed, she was convinced that it was much *more* than enough.

CHAPTER 2

On Their Own

It was a good thing that Aldo's birthday fell in May, close to the end of the school year. Once he became the owner of two frisky puppies, he had hardly any time for school or homework. Dog care was a full-time job.

And watching over Aldo taking care of the puppies was a full-time job for Mrs. Sossi, too. Aldo's father had a two-week business trip to San Francisco coming up at the beginning of July. He wanted his wife to accompany him.

"Who will take care of the kids?" asked Mrs. Sossi.

"Kids? I'm not a kid," protested Elaine. "There's only one kid around here, and that's Aldo. I can take care of him."

"Ordinarily I might agree with you," said her mother. "But this year it's much more complicated than just taking care of yourselves. Peanut and Butter need constant attention. I wouldn't feel comfortable going off and leaving you three alone with the puppies. Who knows what sort of mischief they'll get into?"

She was thinking of some of the mischief they had already accomplished. There was the chewing up of one of Elaine's tennis shoes. Or the afternoon when Peanut had pulled the cloth off the dining room table and broken the vase that had been on it. There was the constant lookout for puddles or damp patches where puddles or damp patches should not have been.

"Thousands of people have dogs. Millions of people have dogs," said Elaine. "They manage. We can manage, too."

"There are forty million dogs in the United States," Aldo chimed in. He had been reading a lot about dogs these days and knew all sorts of canine trivia.

"I could be in charge of the meals if you went away with Dad," Karen offered. She loved cooking, and her cooking was first-rate.

Mrs. Sossi shook her head. "No," she said to her husband and her children. "Another time, perhaps. But this summer I feel I should be on hand to supervise."

So the school year ended, and Mr. Sossi began packing for his trip. Mrs. Sossi was staying home; that was the plan. But at seven o'clock on the morning after Mr. Sossi's departure, the telephone rang. It was unusual to get a call so early in the day. Mrs. Sossi was in the shower. Elaine and Karen and Aldo were still asleep, or at least still half-asleep. They all enjoyed staying in bed, now that they didn't have to get up early to go off to school. It was Elaine who jumped out of bed to answer the phone.

"Mom," she called in a loud voice. "Mom!"

Aldo got out of bed and knocked on the bathroom door. "Mom," he shouted above the sound of running water. "There's a telephone call for you."

The water stopped, and a moment later Mrs. Sossi emerged, wearing her terry-cloth robe. Water was dripping from her hair. "What is it?" she asked anxiously.

"It's Grandma," Elaine called out. "She says that Grandpa had an emergency operation in the middle of the night."

Mrs. Sossi grabbed the phone to speak with her mother. Her face, which had been flushed when she got out of the shower, turned pale as she listened to the voice on the other end.

"What does the doctor say?" she asked.

Aldo, Elaine, and Karen stood around her. They, too, wondered what the doctor said.

"I'll come at once," said Mrs. Sossi. "I'll call the airlines right now and take the first flight that I can get. Don't worry," she told her mother. But it was quite obvious that, despite her words, Mrs. Sossi was very worried.

"Your grandfather is very ill," she said when she got off the phone. "I have to go see him." She looked around at her children. "Can you manage for just a few days on your own?"

"Of course we can," said Elaine.

No one said a word about the dogs who were barking downstairs. They wanted their morning walk and they wanted their breakfast. Dogs didn't understand about emergency phone calls and things like that.

And so, by ten minutes past eight that morning, it was all arranged. Mrs. Sossi, who had felt so strongly that she should remain at home while her husband was away, had an eleven o'clock reservation to fly to Florida. Aldo, Karen, Elaine, Peabody, Peanut, and Butter were going to be on their own after all.

It was only ten minutes past five in the morning in San Francisco, so Mrs. Sossi postponed phoning her husband to tell him these new plans. But she called Mrs. Lorin, who lived just a couple of houses away. "She can keep an eye on you," said Mrs. Sossi.

"Oh, Mom. We don't need anyone looking after us," complained Elaine, even though Mrs. Lorin was the mother of her best friend, Sandy.

By nine-thirty, Mrs. Sossi had packed a small

suitcase and left. It was a strange sensation. Of course Elaine and Karen and Aldo were concerned about their grandfather's health. Still, even as they worried about their grandfather, the three younger Sossis were excited by this unexpected chance for independence. It wasn't every day that both your parents left town!

"We're going to have a super time," said Elaine. "And we're going to show Mom and Dad that we can manage just fine."

Aldo could see that she was bursting with the importance of being the oldest and therefore in charge of the situation.

The phone rang, and Elaine rushed to answer it. Perhaps their grandfather's condition had gotten worse.

"Oh, hi, Mrs. Lorin," Elaine said into the receiver. Both Aldo and Karen relaxed. It wasn't a bulletin from the hospital. It was only their neighbor. Probably she was just checking up that their mother had left on schedule.

"Oh, sure. We'd love to come to dinner at your house," Elaine said. "We'll be there. Thanks."

Elaine hung up the phone. "Mrs. Lorin just invited us to come for supper tonight," she said.

"You had no right to accept an invitation without asking us," complained Karen. "Suppose we didn't want to go. I don't need anyone to cook for me. I can cook for myself. And I can cook for all of us."

"I'm in charge, remember," said Elaine. "It was very nice of Mrs. Lorin to ask us over, especially since Mom only called her a little while ago and told her about the situation here."

"Just because you're the oldest doesn't mean that you can boss us around," said Karen. "I'm not going to the Lorins'. You can go without me." She turned to her brother. "Are you going to stay home and have supper with me?"

Aldo wished his mother was there to help him out. He hated having to make decisions that resulted in one sister being angry at him while the other was pleased with him.

"I think we should all stick together," he said. "Can't we eat at the Lorins' tonight and make a plan that, no matter who else calls, tomorrow we'll eat here? And if we get any other invitations, we'll talk about them before we accept. Sometimes Mom and Dad accept invitations for the whole family, but lots of other times just one of us goes off to a friend's house."

Then he had a great idea. "Why don't you make a cake or something to bring to the Lorins'?" he suggested to Karen.

Karen's expression changed. "I have a fantastic book of chocolate recipes that I took out of the library. I could make one of those cakes," she offered.

"Oh, yes," said Elaine. "That's a super idea." She looked over at Aldo and smiled at him. The first crisis had been averted.

The rest of the day passed uneventfully. Aldo walked Peanut and Butter. They didn't seem to be aware that the elder Sossis had left the scene. The dogs were their usual lively selves.

Aldo took advantage of the fact that his parents weren't home to permit the dogs out of the kitchen area, where they were generally penned in these days. It must be awfully boring for them, he thought. Imagine having to spend all your time indoors inside the kitchen.

He tried once again to put his training program into effect. According to one of the books he had gotten from the library, he was supposed to speak firmly to the dogs and give them commands.

"Stay!" he would shout to Peanut, but Peanut wouldn't stay.

"Sit," he told Butter. He pushed the dog into a sitting position as the book told him to do.

Butter seemed to think it was a game. Immediately she jumped back up, like a toy on a spring.

Aldo wondered if he would ever be able to teach the dogs anything.

Karen's chocolate cake was a work of art. Sandy Lorin and her parents were full of admiration. So the evening meal passed pleasantly.

Sandy Lorin had adopted one of the surplus birthday puppies that Aldo had received. Although he and Sandy had often met while walking their puppies on the street, this was the first chance Aldo had had to compare notes. Sandy had named her dog Mischief. Aldo could see that the name was appropriate. The pup was as naughty as Peanut and Butter put together.

Aldo shared some of his growing knowledge about dogs with the Lorin family. "Did you know that the largest dog on record weighed two hundred ninety-five pounds?" he asked.

"Two hundred ninety-five pounds of mischief. I couldn't take that," groaned Mrs. Lorin.

After supper, they all sat around the Lorins' television and watched a film together. It was *The Invasion of the Body Snatchers*. It was a scary movie. Half the time Karen and Elaine and Sandy covered their eyes and shrieked. Aldo thought they were acting silly. Especially after he noticed that they always peeked through their fingers when they pretended to cover their eyes. Still, they laughed a lot, too, and so it was a very pleasant evening, and everyone had a good time. Even Karen, who wouldn't have admitted it for the world, or at least not in front of Elaine, enjoyed herself.

It was after ten o'clock when Aldo and his sisters returned to their home. Karen and Elaine went inside, and Aldo gave the puppies their evening walk. Peanut broke loose and ran, trailing her leash behind her as she crossed the yard next door and tore down the street. Aldo ran after her, pulling Butter

behind him. It took him about fifteen minutes to retrieve the runaway dog. He was quite exhausted when he finally took the puppies back inside the house.

Then he stood outside, clapping his hands for Peabody. It was his signal for the cat to return home for the night. On most nights during the year, the cat promptly appeared. It was one of the few tricks that Aldo had succeeded in teaching him. However, on warm summer evenings, the cat seemed to forget this game. Sometimes Aldo found him sleeping in a dark corner of the lawn.

After several minutes of clapping, Peabody slowly emerged from behind a bush. He wasn't in a hurry to come inside. Aldo stood quietly until the cat came near. Then he scooped Peabody up into his arms.

"Time for bed," he told the cat. It was a silly thing to say to the animal, since he had probably just awakened from a nap.

"Dad called," Karen reported to Aldo when he entered the living room. "Mom phoned him and said that Grandpa's operation was a success. The next twenty-four hours are critical, but there were no complications. Dad sends his love and says he knows we'll be okay on our own."

"Of course we'll be all right," said Elaine. She turned to Aldo. "Did you lock the door when you came inside?"

"I think so," said Aldo.

"Go and check," Elaine instructed him. "This is our first night on our own, and I don't want anyone breaking in." As she spoke, she went from window to window in the living room, checking that each was locked.

"Are you scared?" asked Karen.

"Of course not. Are you?" asked Elaine.

"What's to be scared of?" asked Aldo, returning from the front door.

"Nothing," said Elaine. "But this is the first time we ever slept alone in the house. And it's hard to be in charge when you are sound asleep."

"You don't have to be in charge while you're sleeping," said Aldo.

"Someone *has* to be in charge," said Elaine. "Did you notice how dark it is outside?"

"It's always dark at night," said Aldo.

"Well, it looks darker than usual to me," said Elaine. "I think we should keep a couple of lights on during the night—just in case."

"In case of what?" asked Aldo. "Peanut and Butter won't understand that it's nighttime if we leave the lights on in the house."

"It's better if they stay awake," said Elaine. "Then they can act as watchdogs."

"That's a good idea," Karen agreed.

"Are you scared, too?" asked Aldo. He couldn't believe that his sisters were talking this way about the dark.

"I'm not scared—just cautious. We usually have Mom and Dad to keep an eye on things. It's good to know that the dogs will be here in case anyone tries to enter the house."

"I locked the door," Aldo reminded her. "The windows are locked, too. No one is going to come in."

"I wish we hadn't just seen that movie," admitted Karen, looking at one of her mother's plants on a nearby table.

"Yikes!" shrieked Elaine. "I have a couple of plants in my bedroom. I'm going to take them out right now," she said, remembering how the plants in the film had grown during the night and encircled the bodies of the sleeping people.

"You two are crazy," said Aldo, yawning. "I'm going to sleep and I'm turning the light out in my room. You can keep your lights on if you want, but don't leave any lights on downstairs. Peanut and Butter need their sleep. They'll wake up if anyone tries to enter the house. And besides, I read that dogs have great night vision, just like cats. So they won't need your electric lights."

"Would you like to sleep in my room with me?" Elaine said to Karen.

"Sure," said Karen, quickly accepting the invitation.

Aldo laughed as he put on his pajamas. He remembered how thrilled his sisters had been last year when they had moved to this new home of theirs in Woodside. Now each had her own room and didn't have to share the same space. They had been delighted with their privacy. But he guessed that they only wanted privacy when the sun was shining or their parents were home to watch over them.

As he got into bed, he thought about Peabody.

The cat certainly wasn't afraid of the night. Peabody knew that there was nothing evil or frightening outside. If Aldo had let him, Peabody would have spent the entire night outdoors.

It wasn't until the following morning, when the sun was shining brightly, that Aldo, Karen, and Elaine Sossi discovered that somebody or something had indeed been lurking outside their house the night before.

CHAPTER 3

Mrs. Crosby
Gets Cross

At seven-thirty the next morning, Aldo lay in bed half-awake. He knew that he had to get up and give the puppies their morning walk. Still, he turned over into a more comfortable position and remained in bed. The puppies, who were downstairs in the kitchen, were probably asleep, because they were not making any noise.

Then the telephone rang. Aldo jumped out of bed.

"Maybe it's Mom," shouted Karen.

"Maybe there's news about Grandpa," shouted Elaine.

Peanut and Butter heard the phone and the voices and began barking.

"I've got it," shouted Aldo, picking up the receiver.

"Hello?" he said.

"Mrs. Sossi?" said a voice at the other end.

"No, this is Aldo," he said. How embarrassing to be mistaken for your mother on the telephone.

"This is Mrs. Crosby from next door. Tell your parents to come over to my house immediately. I want them to see the condition of my front yard."

"Who is it?" asked Elaine.

"Is Grandpa all right?" asked Karen.

Aldo shook his head and gestured to his sisters to keep quiet. "My parents aren't home," he said. He wondered why Mrs. Crosby wanted them to look at her yard anyhow. It seemed a very silly request so early in the morning.

"Then you had better come over here yourself at once, young man," she said.

"Me?" asked Aldo.

"Yes, you. You'll see why soon enough," she said, and hung up. Mrs. Crosby sounded pretty angry, and Aldo couldn't imagine what had happened to annoy her.

"What is it?" asked Elaine. "Why didn't you put me on the phone?"

"It was Mrs. Crosby. I don't know what she's so cross about, but she said I should come right over and see her yard."

"Her yard? That's weird," said Karen.

"I know," said Aldo as he pulled a T-shirt over his head and looked for the jeans that he had dropped on the floor the night before.

In the year and a half they had lived here, the family had had only good relations with their next-door neighbor, who was a widow and lived alone. Sometimes Mrs. Sossi had run errands for her, and Mr. Sossi had removed her storm windows in the spring and hung her screens. At Halloween, Mrs. Crosby had been generous with her candy hand-outs, and during the winter, when there was a big snowstorm, Aldo had shoveled her walk for her. Why was she sounding so angry on the telephone now, he wondered. Peanut and Butter hadn't been barking in the night. She couldn't say that they kept her awake. Besides, why would she want him to come and look at her yard? It didn't make any sense.

Nor did it make sense to Peanut and Butter. Ever since the phone had rung, the dogs had been whining for attention. Now, seeing Aldo, they set up a terrific barking. The phone was ringing again, too. Aldo was tempted to stay and hear who it was. But he was afraid it might be Mrs. Crosby asking what was taking him so long. He hurried to the door.

Peabody was waiting for his breakfast, too. Aldo bent down and gave the cat a quick pat. "I'll feed you in a couple of minutes," he told the animal. Peabody meowed his complaint as he followed Aldo outside. He wanted his breakfast right now.

Mrs. Crosby was waiting in front of her house. "Just look at this," she said, pointing to her lawn. Instead of the green grass that had been in front of the house the day before, there were now large patches of exposed dirt where clumps of grass had been dug up. It was a mess.

"Gee," said Aldo. "What happened?"

"What happened? I'll tell you what happened," said Mrs. Crosby, getting red in the face. "One of your animals has dug up my lawn."

"My dogs are always on a leash," said Aldo. "So they couldn't have done this. And Peabody would never do a thing like this. I know he didn't do it."

"Oh, you do, do you. I've seen your cat walking across my lawn almost every day since you moved here. And I've seen your dogs running here, too. I never had a reason to complain about it until now. But this is dreadful." She stopped speaking for a moment, and Aldo followed her gaze. "Look," she said.

Peabody had walked over from Aldo's house and was making his way across Mrs. Crosby's lawn. The cat approached Aldo and began rubbing his body against Aldo's ankles.

Aldo bent down and picked up his cat. He knew that Mrs. Crosby thought that Peabody was returning to the scene of his crime. The cat was just plain hungry. And now that he thought about it, Aldo felt his own stomach was waiting for some food.

"You may not know it, but I'm trying to rent my house," said Mrs. Crosby. "I'm expecting several people to come look at it today. How do you think this is going to appear to them?"

Aldo put Peabody down on the ground. "You have a very nice house," he said politely. "If people come to look at it, they aren't going to care about your grass."

"Of course they are going to care. It's the very first thing they'll see, and first impressions are very important."

"Well, Peabody did not do it," said Aldo. "He never did a thing like this before, so it doesn't make any sense that, out of the blue, he would do it now."

"Then it must have been your dogs," asserted Mrs. Crosby.

"None of my pets did this," said Aldo, looking at his neighbor. Although he was angry at her for blaming the Sossi pets for this mess in the yard, he also began to feel sorry for her. She looked as if she was about to start crying. He wondered how it felt to live all alone. Maybe she was scared in the night, like his sisters.

"I know they didn't do it," Aldo repeated. "But if you wait until I walk my dogs and feed them some breakfast, I'll come try and fix up this mess for you."

"All right," said Mrs. Crosby. "But hurry. The first real estate agent is bringing a couple here to see the house at ten o'clock."

Aldo walked back to his house with Peabody at his heels. "You'll never believe what's bothering Mrs. Crosby," he told his sisters as he opened up a can of food for the cat.

"Do you think it's possible that Peabody did it?" asked Karen after she heard about their neighbor's complaint.

"Of course not," shouted Aldo. It was bad enough that Mrs. Crosby was suspicious of Peabody. How could his own sister say a thing like that?

"Could Peanut or Butter have done it?" asked Elaine.

"That's a stupid question," said Aldo. "You know they are always on their leashes. How could either of them dig up Mrs. Crosby's lawn?"

As he waited for Elaine to come up with a solution to his question, Aldo came up with the answer himself. He remembered that, the night before, Peanut had broken loose from him and had run off toward Mrs. Crosby's yard. Could she have dug up the grass before Aldo caught her? It had been dark. Aldo hadn't noticed anything.

Peanut and Butter were barking madly. They had never had to wait so long for their morning walk and breakfast.

Aldo went to the cupboard and removed the bag of dog food. He poured some into each dog's bowl and added just the right amount of water to moisten it. It was not easy to do with both dogs jumping at his legs and pulling on his jeans. One would think it was days and not hours since they were last fed. After the puppies gulped down their food, Aldo went to get the leashes. He walked with the dogs in the direction away from Mrs. Crosby's house so he wouldn't have to look at her lawn.

When he finished walking the dogs, he took his mother's small garden trowel and returned to the house next door.

As he replaced each of the dug-up clumps of grass on Mrs. Crosby's lawn, patting each one back into place so you could hardly see the damage of the night before, Aldo wondered how he could convince his neighbor that none of his pets was the villain.

Perhaps some kid had come along in the night and done it for a joke. They had discussed vandalism in school. It was senseless, but it happened from time to time. Someone had spray-painted the front of the elementary school building a few months ago.

While Aldo was working, Peabody appeared and stood next to him. Karen or Elaine must have let the cat out of the house. "Get away from here. Stop watching me," Aldo hissed at the cat. "You don't want Mrs. Crosby to see you on her grass. You're one of the prime suspects."

Peabody ignored Aldo and began sniffing the grass. Aldo looked up and, sure enough, saw Mrs. Crosby watching them from her front window. He made a grab for Peabody and, lifting him up, carried him off in the direction of the Sossi house.

"You have to stay away from Mrs. Crosby's lawn," he scolded the cat. He examined Peabody's paws. Surely there would be dirt on them if he had done any digging. But the cat's feet were pink and clean. Too bad you can't take fingerprints from a cat to prove its innocence, he thought.

"Peabody may have washed away all the evidence," said Karen, who had come outside and saw Aldo inspecting his pet's paws. "Cats are very clean animals—unlike dogs."

Aldo guessed her meaning. "Did one of the puppies have another accident?" asked Aldo.

"Yep." She giggled.

Aldo sighed. "At least Mom isn't home to get upset about it."

"Come on inside," urged Karen. "You must be starving. I made some pancakes for breakfast."

Aldo stood up and brushed the dirt from his hands. He handed the trowel to Karen and lifted up Peabody. "I'm going to make him stay inside all day," he said. "Then if anything happens to Mrs. Crosby's lawn again, she can't blame him."

"Good idea," agreed Karen, leading the way into the house.

Aldo washed his hands and sat down at the dining room table, where a stack of pancakes was waiting for him. Peanut and Butter were jumping around at his legs.

"Take it easy," he said to the dogs. "You already had *your* breakfast."

Butter tried to jump up onto Aldo's lap. As she did, she jiggled his arm, and the bottle of pancake syrup that he was holding fell out of his grasp. Miraculously, it missed Aldo's lap, but the bottle spilled all over the dog.

"Oh, no," moaned Aldo.

"Is something wrong with my pancakes?" called Karen from the kitchen.

"I don't know. I haven't eaten any yet," said Aldo. The sticky syrup was all over the dog. Despite himself, Aldo began to giggle. There was one brand of pancake syrup which advertised that it was flavored with butter. Here was Butter flavored with syrup. Every one of her short hairs was coated with it.

Aldo jumped up and tried to grab the sticky dog. But Butter ran under the table and into the living room. "Get me some wet towels," he shouted to Karen.

"Another accident?" she asked as she brought them to him.

"Another sort of accident," he said. He pulled Butter out from behind the living room curtains and

tried to clean her off. But he could see that she needed more than a sponge bath. DeDe had offered to help him bathe the dogs when they got a bit older. But Aldo didn't think he could wait that long. He went to the phone and called his friend at once.

CHAPTER 4

Puppy Kisses

DeDe promised to come over right after lunch. The thought cheered Aldo, but only slightly. This was not turning out to be a good day at all.

"Mom called while you were outside," Elaine reported to Aldo as she came down the stairs. "Grandpa is still in critical condition. He's in the intensive care unit at the hospital. She said she won't be home for at least a week."

Aldo nodded glumly. He had thought that, by this morning, his grandfather would be better. Even though his grandparents lived a great distance away and he didn't see them often, Aldo cared a lot about

■ 44 ■

them. His grandfather shared Aldo's love of animals. Every year he sent Aldo a calendar with beautiful photographs of animals. The July page hanging in Aldo's room showed a mother swan and two cygnets. Aldo hoped that, by the time he turned the calendar to August (which showed a pair of adult giraffes and their babies), his grandfather would be out of the hospital and fully recovered.

"Okay, you guys. I'll see you at lunchtime," Elaine announced. "I'm going off to play tennis with Scott."

"I should have guessed from your outfit," said Karen. Elaine was wearing a pair of white shorts and a white T-shirt. "The only thing is, you don't know how to play tennis."

"Scott is going to teach me," said Elaine as she went out the door to meet her boyfriend.

"Hey, Aldo," said Karen as the door closed behind their sister. "I was looking at one of the books about dog care that you took out of the library. I found a recipe for Puppy Kisses. I thought I'd make a batch this morning."

"Puppy Kisses?" said Aldo. He thought of the wet licks both Peanut and Butter gave him all over his face and hands whenever they had a chance. "Are Puppy Kisses for puppies or people?"

"They're for puppies, of course. See. Here's the recipe."

Aldo took the library book and looked at the page that Karen was pointing to. Sure enough, there was a recipe for a treat for dogs. "Reward your pet for good behavior with one of these special and healthy snacks," it said. The recipe called for beef hearts or kidneys chopped fine and mixed with flour and a little cooking oil.

"Do you really think they'll like them?" asked Aldo. He wouldn't want to eat anything like that.

"What don't these puppies like to eat?" asked Karen.

She was right. Look how they had licked up the spilled syrup this morning. And Aldo always had to be careful to keep Peabody's cat food out of their reach or they would eat that, too. And when they didn't eat, they chewed—on shoes, books, flowers, chair legs, etc.

"I'll ride down to the butcher on my bike and get a beef heart," said Karen. "I'll be back in a few minutes."

While Karen was gone, Aldo walked about the living room and, with damp paper towels, tried to clean it up a little. The coffee table, the chairs, the rug—everything felt sticky to him. But it was a futile task because Butter was still sticky. And even if he managed to clean up the room, the dog quickly made things sticky all over again. So Aldo put the chore off until another day.

Peabody, who had been upstairs, came down and stood at the doorway meowing. He wanted to go outside. But Aldo was afraid to let the cat out. Peanut and Butter wanted to play with Peabody, but that was not the cat's idea of fun. His tail grew fat and his hair stood up as the puppies approached him. Aldo wondered how long it would be until Peabody felt comfortable in the presence of the dogs.

Karen returned, proudly bearing the meat that she needed.

"I don't want to see," said Aldo when she offered to show him the beef heart she had bought.

"How can you study to be a veterinarian if you are going to be squeamish," she teased him.

Aldo wondered about that himself, but luckily he

had many years before he would have to worry. So he stayed out of the kitchen while Karen chopped the meat into tiny pieces. However, Peanut and Butter jumped about at her feet. They weren't squeamish at all. They were, as always, curious and hungry.

In a little while, Karen put the first batch of Puppy Kisses into the oven. When they finished baking, she brought the cookie tray over for Aldo to admire. He saw sixteen lightly browned wafers. They resembled a type of hazelnut cookie that Karen had made last year at Christmas time.

"Do you want to try one?" offered Karen.

"I'm not a puppy," said Aldo. "Besides, they have meat in them."

"Ooops. Sorry about that. I forgot," said Karen.

But when the kisses had cooled, she gave one to each of the dogs.

"They love them," said Karen proudly, as the dogs munched their little home-baked treats.

When they had finished eating, it was time for Aldo to take Peanut and Butter for their midmorning walk. Remembering how Peanut had escaped the night before, Aldo asked Karen if she would help him. So they each took a leash and a dog and went outside.

"Maybe I can find some more dog recipes," said Karen as Butter pulled her along the street.

Forty-five minutes later, when Aldo and Karen returned home, they found Elaine and Scott sprawled on the living room floor. Their tennis rackets lay beside them.

"Hi," Aldo greeted his sister and her boyfriend.

"Hi," Elaine said. She turned to Karen. "We've been eating your cookies. I don't think they're up to your usual standard. They're nice and crunchy, but I found them kind of bland. So I had a great idea. I sprinkled cinnamon and sugar on them, and that improves them one hundred percent. Bet you didn't think I could do anything in the kitchen, but sometimes I can come up with a good culinary idea, too."

"You ate those kisses I made?" asked Karen.

"Well, not all of them. I only had three or four. And Scott had some, too. Playing tennis really gives you an appetite. There are still some left for you."

"They were good, Karen," said Scott, smiling. "You don't mind that we ate them, do you?"

"I guess not. I can always make some more for the dogs."

"For the dogs!" said both Elaine and Scott in unison.

"What do you mean? What was inside them?" asked Elaine, starting to gag.

Karen laughed. "It's a very romantic recipe. There's a chopped beef heart in the recipe. I found it in one of Aldo's library books about dog care. They're called Puppy Kisses. And they're meant especially for dogs. It's to reward them for good behavior."

"I feel sick," said Elaine. "I think I'll die. I know I'll die."

"From embarrassment, not from my cooking," Karen said, laughing. "I can't wait for Mom and Dad to call home again so I can tell them."

Aldo grinned at his sister. It was just like Elaine to eat the dog biscuits that Karen had baked.

"I've only one thing to say," said Scott as he got up to leave.

"What's that?" asked Elaine in a weak voice.

"Bowwow, bowwow," said Scott.

Wet Dogs and Green Lobsters

"I want to cook something super special for to-night," said Karen as she and Aldo and Elaine fin-ished eating a lunch of cheese sandwiches and cherry tomatoes.

"Like what?" asked Aldo, swallowing the last of his milk.

"I don't know," said Karen. "But don't worry. Whatever I make, there'll be something without meat on the menu."

"That's okay," said Aldo. "I could eat a bowl of cornflakes if I don't want your supper."

Karen went off on her bike to go shopping for dinner.

"Sandy's coming over," Elaine reported to Aldo.

"DeDe is coming here, too," said Aldo. "We're going to give the dogs a bath." Somehow, even though the syrup had spilled on Butter, Peanut had also gotten pretty sticky. So Aldo had decided that the dogs should be bathed together.

"That sounds messy to me," said Elaine.

"It's all right," said Aldo. "We're going to do it outdoors. And besides," he added, "DeDe is very experienced, since she has a dog of her own at home. She's done it loads of times."

Sandy Lorin arrived, and she and Elaine locked themselves into Elaine's bedroom. Aldo could hear them giggling together as he took some large bath towels out of the linen closet. He wanted to have everything ready when DeDe came. A few minutes later DeDe arrived. She was carrying something made out of plastic.

"It's a deflated wading pool. I used to play in it when I was a baby. Now it's perfect for a dog bath."

They took the pool out to the backyard, and Aldo located the bicycle pump in the garage. He and

DeDe took turns until the pool was finally filled with air and ready to be filled with water from the garden hose.

Then at last, the big moment arrived. Peanut and Butter were brought outside and placed into the water. Both dogs began barking. But whether they were barking because they enjoyed the water or because they didn't like it, Aldo couldn't tell.

With one arm around Peanut to keep her from jumping out of the pool, Aldo felt about in the water for the bar of soap. Once he located it, he began to rub it on the dog's fur.

"Give me the soap, too," said DeDe.

Aldo held the soap out to her, and DeDe started to lather up Butter. "With all the soapsuds on them, they are matching dogs." DeDe laughed.

It was true. Aldo leaned back to get a good look at both dogs together, and suddenly Peanut jumped out of his grasp. The dog was delighted that she was not attached to a leash. She charged through the yard, and Aldo ran after her.

Aldo was always amazed how fast his dogs could run. Peanut raced to the front of the house. A car had just pulled up in front of Mrs. Crosby's house, and two women and a man got out. The puppy ran toward them.

"Help!" shrieked one of the women.

"She won't hurt you," shouted Aldo.

Peanut stood still for a moment, looking at all these new people. Then she gave herself a hard shake so that water and soapsuds went flying from her. Some of the water landed on the people who had come to view Mrs. Crosby's house. Aldo tried to make a grab for Peanut. But the dog's fur was so soapy that she was too slippery for him. Peanut escaped Aldo's hold and started running down the street.

"Peanut! Sit!" Aldo shouted. But Peanut had never been one for sitting. She just kept running. Aldo ran, too, but he tripped and fell before he got more than a couple of yards.

Luckily, at just that moment, Karen was returning down the street on her bike. She jumped off her bike and made a grab for the dog.

"It's a good thing I didn't buy any eggs," she said as she handed over the wet and wriggling animal to her brother. Karen's bike had crashed onto the street as she jumped off. Several of her grocery items

had fallen out of the basket. But nothing looked damaged except Aldo. He had scraped his chin when he fell.

Aldo put his hand through Peanut's collar to be sure he had a good hold on the dog. He walked slowly back to the yard, where DeDe was calmly rubbing Butter dry with one of the towels. She made the process of giving a dog a bath look very easy. But now Aldo knew otherwise.

"I didn't try to help you catch Peanut because Butter would have run off, too," she explained.

Aldo put Peanut back into the baby pool and splashed water on her to rinse off the soap. He heard the slam of a car door and the sound of a car driving away.

"I hope Mrs. Crosby didn't lose a chance to rent her house because of Peanut," he said.

When the dogs were dry, Aldo and DeDe took them inside. Karen was in the kitchen admiring her purchases. "Look what I bought," she said. "They were having a big sale."

"Lobsters!" shrieked DeDe. "Lucky you. I love lobster. My father takes me to a fish restaurant sometimes when I spend the weekend with him. But they are always red when I see them," she said, admiring the dark green creatures on the kitchen counter.

"These will turn red when they are cooked," said Karen.

"Look. He's moving. Poor thing," said Aldo, watching as one of the lobsters tried to make its way across the counter. "Karen, how can you kill them? You'll be a murderer," said Aldo angrily.

"Don't be silly," said Karen. "The supermarket here in Woodside sells hundreds of lobsters. And all the other supermarkets around the world sell them, too. Millions of people eat them. Just because you don't want to doesn't make me a murderer."

"Yes, it does," said Aldo. "These lobsters aren't just going to lie down and die so you can eat them."

"Aldo, if people didn't eat lobsters, there would be too many lobsters in the sea. They would take up so much room that boats wouldn't be able to move. Eating lobsters is a public service for the shipping industry," claimed Karen. "Besides, I never cooked lobsters before. I just couldn't resist buying them."

"And they taste good, too," DeDe added.

"The man at the fish counter in the supermarket said to put them into the refrigerator until I'm ready to cook them," said Karen.

Aldo shuddered. He hated the idea of harming any animal. He didn't even permit anyone in his family to kill a spider if he was around.

"It's too cold in the refrigerator," he said. "Let them at least spend their last hours swimming."

"Swimming," said Karen. "Where are they going to swim?"

"We can dump the soapy water out of the wading pool and put in clean water."

"My mother said I had to bring the wading pool back home as soon as we finished bathing the dogs. She promised to bring it over to a friend who has a little kid," said DeDe.

"We could put them upstairs in the bathtub," suggested Aldo.

"All right," agreed Karen. "That would be okay with me. But it's just until I'm ready to cook them, Aldo," she warned her brother.

DeDe went outside to empty the wading pool so she could take it home again. Aldo picked up a lobster in each hand and started up the stairs toward the bathroom. Suddenly he heard a loud scream. He was so startled that he almost dropped the lobsters.

"I'll die," a voice shouted. It was Elaine.

"You are dyed," said Sandy, trying to stifle a giggle.

Karen came running from the kitchen and stood on the stairs next to Aldo. Together they stared in amazement as their sister walked out of the bathroom and onto the landing.

There was Elaine with a head of bright green hair.

"You look weird," said Aldo. He looked down at the lobsters he was holding. Green was a good color for lobsters. It was not a good color for humans.

"I can't believe this happened to me," moaned Elaine. "We just used a tonal rinse that was supposed to bring out red highlights in my hair. But something went wrong. This isn't my day. First I ate dog food, and now this."

"Wait till Mom sees you," said Karen. "She'll die."

"Won't it wash out?" asked Aldo.

"I don't know. If it doesn't, I'll never go outdoors again in my life."

"It will grow out," said Sandy. "Or you could get your hair cut real short."

"You mean shave my head," said Elaine. She looked at Aldo. "What are you holding?" she asked.

"That's our supper," said Karen. "Aldo's going to give them a farewell swim in our bathtub."

Despite herself, Elaine began to laugh. "Why not?" she said. "The condemned man is always supposed to eat a hearty meal. I guess the condemned woman can eat one, too."

Karen Cooks Dinner

Aldo filled the bathtub with cold water. The lobsters began to swim about. Poor things. In a few hours, they would be swimming in boiling water. Aldo wondered if he could possibly convince Karen and Elaine to give up their dinner.

"Aldo," Elaine called up the stairs.

"What do you want?" Aldo called down to her.

"There isn't a single clean towel in the house. You better do the laundry."

"Why me?" asked Aldo.

"We're going to take turns," Elaine said in a very

bossy voice. "And you just used the last of the towels when you washed the dogs."

Aldo was about to say, "What about you? How many towels did you use when you dyed your hair green?" but he thought better of it. Poor Elaine was upset enough about her hair. He'd do the laundry this time. Next time one of his sisters would have to do it.

As he walked down the stairs, he noticed the table that Karen had already set for their evening meal. She was really enjoying this chance of being in charge of the food situation. The table was set with one of Mrs. Sossi's best cloths. There was a pair of candles in the candlesticks in the center of the table. There was even a vase with roses, which Aldo recognized as having been cut from their own bushes. The table looked as if they were going to have important guests for dinner. It was unfortunate, however, that it was the lobsters who were the guests of honor at the forthcoming meal.

Aldo put the dirty laundry into the washing machine and, while the wash and rinse cycles took place, he went upstairs and observed the lobsters in the bathtub. Then he looked up *lobster* in the old set of encyclopedias that his mother had picked up at a garage sale some months before. It was very interesting. Discovering that lobsters lived in salt water, Aldo ran downstairs for the salt shaker. He emptied its entire contents into the bathtub. Aldo wondered if anyone ever kept lobsters as pets. On the bulletin board in his bedroom, he had a listing that he had cut out of a magazine. It told which animals were legal and which were illegal to keep as pets in New Jersey. It said,

Legal	*Illegal*
ants	alligators
chameleons	badgers
cockatoos	bears
crayfish	chimpanzees
frogs	ducks
guinea pigs	falcons
hamsters	wolves
iguanas	otters
mice	owls
rabbits	raccoons
shrimp	skunks

Lobsters weren't on either side of the list. But, he

wondered, if shrimp and crayfish were legal pets, wouldn't lobsters be considered legal pets, too? Yet even if he was able to convince his sisters to surrender their dinner tonight, the lobsters would probably be too tempting to keep. Aldo remembered the large chocolate rabbit he had gotten for Easter. He had said he would keep it just as it was in its cellophane wrapper. But then he tore the paper just a little at the top corner and nibbled off one of the ears. And gradually the rabbit had disappeared.

Pet lobsters might disappear, too.

Elaine came upstairs and interrupted Aldo's thoughts. "I can hear that the washing machine has stopped running," she said. "It's time to put everything in the dryer."

Aldo stared at his sister. She really looked weird. He wondered how long it would take to get used to her with green hair.

"Don't look at me like that," said Elaine, reading Aldo's thoughts. "Sandy had to go home. But Karen is going to try and help me get my hair back to a normal shade. She has a plan about using vinegar or peroxide or something like that."

An hour later, when Aldo was on his way to take

the laundry out of the dryer, he saw Karen shampooing Elaine's hair in the kitchen sink. How many bottles of shampoo would it take, he wondered. Karen looked up and asked Aldo to bring the lobsters downstairs. The dinner hour was approaching.

Aldo removed the two green fellows from the bathtub. He didn't look them in the eye as he carried them down to the kitchen. He was about to put them on the counter when he got an idea. He removed the wooden pegs that had been set into their claws, so that they could move more freely. And then, instead of putting them on the counter, he put them on the floor. Maybe they would be smart enough and fast enough to escape.

Then he went down to the basement to fold the laundry. Folding towels was easy. The hard job was trying to remember which T-shirts belonged to Elaine and which to Karen. And sorting out his sisters' underwear was impossible. There seemed to be a hundred socks clinging to everything. Aldo experienced a few mild shocks as he folded up the clothing. It was from the static electricity which he had learned about in school. It made him feel as if he was in the middle of a science experiment. He pulled a sock off a T-shirt and hung it on his shoulder. To his amusement, even though he danced around the basement, the sock did not fall off. He took another sock, and another, and pressed them all over his body. Each sock stuck where Aldo put it. Soon he had about two dozen socks attached to himself.

Instead of rolling the socks into balls, he decided to go upstairs and show off this accomplishment to his sisters. As he gathered the laundry together, he heard loud shrieks. The dogs, who had been sleeping in the living room, began barking, too. Aldo ran up the basement steps to investigate.

"Aldo, help!" screamed Karen.

"What is it?" he called, dropping the folded laundry on the floor as he ran into the kitchen.

Karen and Elaine were standing on the kitchen chairs, while the lobsters that Aldo had released crawled about on the floor. Elaine's hair, which was still at least partly green, was dripping down her face. "I'll never go barefoot again in my life," Elaine shrieked. "At least if I had sneakers on, they couldn't get at my toes."

Peanut and Butter were confused. They seemed

afraid of these strange crawling creatures that did not respond to their barks.

"Why don't you pick them up?" asked Aldo. "That's your supper that you are yelling about."

"I'm afraid they'll pinch me," said Karen. "Look at those claws."

"You're afraid of a pinch," said Aldo, "but you're planning to cook them to death. Is that fair?" He pointed to the pot of water on the stove.

"What are we going to do?" whined Elaine. "We can't stay like this all night."

"I'm going to put the laundry away," said Aldo. He picked up the things he had dropped and left his sisters still standing on the chairs.

"Aldo. Come back," screamed Elaine. "Don't be so mean."

"Aldo. Please help us," Karen called.

It was not often that Aldo found himself in such a position of power over both his sisters. He put the towels in the linen closet and dropped the T-shirts and underwear on Karen's bed. Slowly he walked back down the stairs. He had a big, satisfied grin on his face.

"I have an idea," he said. "If you promise not to

eat the lobsters, I'll catch them so you won't get your toes or fingers pinched."

"What will we do with them?" asked Karen.

"I guess you could take them back to the store where you bought them," said Aldo.

"Then someone else will buy them and eat them. That isn't fair," protested Karen.

"But I won't have to witness it," said Aldo. "And the murder won't be committed here in our kitchen." He looked down at the green creatures on the floor. "It's up to you. You make the decision. I'm going to take the dogs for their walk."

"No, Aldo. Don't leave us up here," shouted Elaine as Aldo moved toward the door.

"What's your decision?" asked Aldo.

"We won't eat the lobsters," said Karen softly. "I've made a big salad and I'll fix some macaroni and cheese."

"Okay. It's a deal," said Aldo. He found a paper shopping bag under the sink and deftly picked up first one lobster and then the other. He put them inside the bag.

Karen and Elaine got off their chairs and back down onto the floor.

"Now I'm going to walk the dogs," said Aldo.

"You can't," said Elaine. Now that she wasn't worrying about preventing her toes from a lobster attack, Elaine was taking over her bossy ways again.

"Why can't I?" asked Aldo.

"Look at yourself. What do you have all over your body?"

Aldo looked down. He saw the socks still clinging to him. He had forgotten all about them. He could have removed them. But doing what Elaine wanted him to do would have detracted from his earlier triumph.

"If you can have green hair, I guess I can wear socks in a few new places," he said. He attached the leashes to the dogs' collars and took them outside for their walk.

Who Is the Villain?

Karen complained that macaroni and cheese wasn't the elegant meal she had envisioned.

Elaine sighed. "It's all right. All this hair dyeing and shampooing has given me an appetite. I'll eat anything."

"It's super," said Aldo. He concentrated on the fact that Karen had returned the lobsters. He refused to think where they might be spending the evening.

On the second evening that both Mr. and Mrs. Sossi were away, Karen and Elaine each slept in her own bed. The effects of *The Invasion of the Body*

Snatchers had thankfully worn off. There was nothing to be afraid of.

Aldo slept with Peabody curled up on the foot of his bed. Peanut and Butter slept cuddled together on the living room sofa.

Except for the sound of crickets or an occasional car driving down the street, all was still, inside and out. Everyone got a good night's sleep. It was abruptly broken, however, before seven in the morning when the telephone rang.

Aldo charged out of bed, upsetting Peabody. Elaine and Karen came running from their rooms. Aldo started when he saw Elaine. He had forgotten about her hair with its green streaks.

Elaine grabbed the telephone. "Hello?" she said in a voice full of anxiety. Could their grandfather have had a relapse?

"Oh, no, not again," she said. She handed the phone to Aldo. It was Mrs. Crosby complaining that her lawn had been torn up in the night.

"I know it wasn't my dogs," Aldo protested loudly on the phone. "I watched them very carefully every minute yesterday. And my cat spent the whole day and night inside the house. He even slept on my bed during the night. Somebody else ruined your grass. It was not one of my pets."

"You better come outside and look," Mrs. Crosby told Aldo in a shrill voice that even Karen and Elaine could hear. "Your grass is all torn up this time, too."

Downstairs, Peanut and Butter were barking their morning greetings. But like the day before, Aldo didn't have time to pet them or take them for their walk. As soon as he had some clothing on, he ran outside. Sure enough, the grass around the front of the house was all dug up in clumps. And looking across the way, Aldo could see that Mrs. Crosby's lawn had suffered the same damage.

Who could have done this? Aldo tried to remember if he had seen anything amiss the night before when he had walked the dogs before bedtime. The only trouble was that it had been dark. If someone or something had already torn up the grass, he hadn't been able to see it in the dark. Would he have to keep Peabody inside the house all day every day from now on?

Mrs. Crosby walked over to the front of the Sossi house. "How will I ever rent my house?" she asked mournfully. "The grass looks terrible." She turned to Aldo, and her voice changed to anger. "And yesterday, every time someone came to look at my home, you scared them away with all your animals and the noise they made. Your dog got one woman so wet and angry, she scarcely looked around at all."

Aldo sighed. "I'll fix your grass again." Was this how he was going to spend every morning all summer long? He decided that it wasn't fair to make the animals suffer just because of what happened in the night. So he went back inside to feed Peabody and to get Peanut and Butter. He would give them their breakfast and their walk before he started working on the lawn.

Aldo walked around to the back door. There he noticed that their large rubbish can had been toppled over in the night, too. A paper bag that had been filled with garbage had been split, and out of it poured its contents: old lettuce leaves and eggshells. Aldo wrinkled his nose in distaste. He knew

Elaine or Karen was going to ask him to clean up that mess. Well, he wasn't going to do it.

"Don't let Peabody out of the house today," he instructed his sisters when he went inside. "I still have to prove to Mrs. Crosby that he isn't guilty of that mess on her lawn."

"Then who did it?" asked Elaine. "It's not the sort of thing a kid would do. And none of our neighbors have cats. These animals are right here. No wonder Mrs. Crosby assumes one of them did it."

"They're all innocent until proven guilty," said Karen, loyally defending Aldo's animals. "It's one of the basics of American democracy. We learned all about it in social studies."

"I learned about that, too," said Elaine. "But it only applies to people, not animals."

The ringing of the telephone stopped the discussion. It was Mrs. Sossi calling once again to check on her children. "Don't tell her about Mrs. Crosby's grass," whispered Aldo to Elaine, who was speaking to their mother. He didn't want to give his mother something else to worry about.

Later in the morning, as Aldo repaired Mrs. Crosby's lawn, DeDe appeared.

"What are you doing?" she asked.

Aldo realized that yesterday they had been so involved with the dog baths that he hadn't even told her about the mystery of the destroyed lawn. He explained it now, glad to take a break from the tiring job of patting down the torn-up clumps of grass.

"I'm sure my pets are innocent," he said. "But I can't really prove it."

"I know what," said DeDe excitedly. "We can stay outside tonight and watch secretly. Then we'll find out who really does this."

"That's a great idea," said Aldo, brightening. "We'll be detectives! Would your mother let you do that? Could you really spend the whole night outside?" He realized he was lucky: He wouldn't need to ask his parents, since neither was around to criticize the plan.

"Don't worry," said DeDe. "I'll arrange it." She thought a moment. "We'll have to wear dark clothes," she said, "so we'll blend into the scenery.

We could hide under the shrubbery," she said, pointing to the bushes that separated the Crosby property from that owned by the Sossis.

Elaine shuddered when Aldo told her the plan. "I wouldn't want to spend the whole night outside," she said.

"You better wear a turtleneck shirt with long sleeves so you don't get eaten alive by mosquitoes," suggested Karen.

"Take a flashlight," said Elaine. "When you hear someone digging in the yard, you can recognize who they are."

"Wear boots so you don't get your feet wet from the dew," said Karen. The sisters had a lot of suggestions, but fortunately neither objected to the plan.

DeDe came over to Aldo's house around seven in the evening. She was carrying a flight bag. "This has all my equipment," she said. She pulled out a long-sleeved navy blue sweatshirt. She also had a Polaroid camera that she had borrowed from her mother. "This is so we can get a picture of the villain in action," she said.

"Great thinking," said Aldo with admiration.

"What's this?" he asked, pulling something with a floral print out of DeDe's bag.

DeDe giggled. "That's my nightgown. My mother stuck it in. She thinks I'm sleeping in a bed in Karen's room. I didn't exactly explain the whole thing to her. Parents are such good worriers."

Aldo laughed. He knew exactly what DeDe meant.

It was still quite light outdoors, much too early to begin their detective work. So the two friends played Ping-Pong in Aldo's basement for a while. It wasn't easy. Peabody walked around underfoot meowing his complaints to them. He didn't understand why he had been forced to spend the entire day inside the house.

"Peabody, you've got to be patient," said Aldo as he tripped once more on the cat and missed a return shot of the ball. "If all goes according to our plan, tomorrow you can go outside again." Peabody did not seem satisfied with this answer. He continued to meow.

Aldo and DeDe went upstairs and had a glass of milk and a slice of the cherry pie that Karen had baked. Then they took Peanut and Butter out for their evening walk. It still wasn't really dark when they returned to the Sossi house. But DeDe suggested that they get ready for their evening adventure and sit outside on Aldo's front steps.

"It always seems to get dark all of a sudden, from one minute to the next," she said. "We have to be ready and not miss a moment of darkness."

So they put on their dark sweatshirts. DeDe took the camera. Aldo got a flashlight. He did not put on boots. A detective didn't worry about getting his feet wet. And besides, it would be difficult to move about silently if he was wearing them.

When they sat on the steps, they could still see in the dimming evening light that the grass was in place as Aldo had fixed it that morning.

"When is your mother coming home?" asked DeDe.

Aldo shrugged. "Not for a few more days, I guess. She's waiting for my grandfather to be released from the hospital."

"It must be fun to be all on your own," she said.

"I'm not exactly on my own," Aldo reminded

her. They turned around and saw both Karen and Elaine looking at them from the living room window.

"I think that's a good place to hide," said DeDe softly. She nodded toward a large hydrangea bush a few yards away.

"Should we go now?" whispered Aldo. It was really getting dark.

"Wait a minute," said DeDe. "We don't want anyone to see us."

They sat on the steps as Mr. Lorin walked past the house with Mischief on a leash. Sandy must have taken the night off from her dog-walking responsibilities. When Mr. Lorin was out of sight, DeDe gave the signal.

"Let's go," she said, leading the way. In a moment, both Aldo and DeDe were sitting under the bush.

A little later, they heard footsteps as Mr. Lorin and Mischief returned and passed the house on their way home. It made Aldo want to laugh, knowing that he was able to see what was going on in the street but no one could see him.

"Isn't this fun?" whispered DeDe into Aldo's ear. "Maybe I'll work for the FBI when I grow up."

After a while, it wasn't as much fun. The ground began to feel damp, and Aldo's jeans stuck to him. Mosquitoes buzzed around them, and Aldo found himself scratching his face and neck. When the back of his hand began to itch, too, he turned on the flashlight for a moment to inspect it. Sure enough, a red welt showed that he had a large mosquito bite.

"Hey, turn that off," hissed DeDe. "Do you want to give away our hiding place?"

At that very moment, DeDe sneezed. Aldo giggled. "Now who's giving away our hiding place?" he asked.

"Shh," whispered DeDe sternly. "We've got to keep quiet if we're going to succeed."

So they sat waiting. An occasional car passed down the street. In the distance, they could hear a baby crying. Otherwise, all was still.

Maybe the vandal was going to take the evening off. Perhaps they would stay outside all night long and not find anything.

Suddenly, DeDe grabbed Aldo's sleeve. "I think I hear something."

Aldo listened intently in the dark. There was the sound of something moving in the grass nearby. He looked about. "Look over there," he said.

In the dark, they could make out the figure of an animal the size of a dog slowly walking across the lawn. They watched as the animal stopped and began to dig in the soil. "See? I knew it wasn't Peabody," whispered Aldo.

DeDe slid forward on her stomach, holding the camera in front of her. She pushed the button that would activate the flash. "Hurry up," she whispered impatiently to the camera.

A tiny red light came on, and at the same moment DeDe pressed the shutter. There was an instant of light as the picture was taken. It was so fast that Aldo didn't even have time to focus his eyes. DeDe pulled off the first damp photo and handed it to Aldo. Then she immediately took a second and a third picture. Aldo held the unfinished pictures in his hand as he crept closer to the animal. Whatever the animal was doing, the moments of light didn't seem to disturb it.

Aldo aimed the flashlight directly on the animal, which was now only a few feet away. He wanted to see what the dog looked like. Did it have a collar? Was it a stray? To his and DeDe's amazement, it was not a dog digging in the grass. It was a full-grown raccoon.

Mr. Sossi
Phones Home

When the telephone rang the next morning, it woke
Aldo, Elaine, Karen, and DeDe. The latter had
changed into her flowered nightgown and had slept
in Karen's room after she and Aldo had gone inside
the house the night before.

Aldo jumped out of bed and ran for the phone.

"Hello, Mrs. Crosby," he said before their neighbor even had a chance to identify herself. "Yes, I
know your lawn is all dug up again. This time I
know who did it."

Once they had photographed the raccoon in action, Aldo and DeDe had chased it away. But Aldo

was not surprised to hear that the raccoon had returned again later in the night. Before he had gone to sleep, he had read the entry under *raccoon* in the encyclopedia. He had learned that raccoons are stubborn and clever animals. They eat all sorts of foods, including insects and grubs. Obviously, the animal they had seen was digging up his supper. It also explained the overturned rubbish can that he had discovered the day before.

"I'll be right over," said Aldo to Mrs. Crosby. For the third morning in a row, he quickly dressed and ran out of the house, leaving the puppies barking demands for their breakfast and their walk.

DeDe came, too. She was clutching the pictures she had taken.

"Look," said Aldo proudly. "Now you can see that my animals didn't do anything to your lawn. It's this raccoon. We took these pictures of him last night."

Mrs. Crosby studied the pictures. "That's a raccoon, all right," she agreed. She turned to Aldo and put her arm around him. "I am terribly sorry that I kept scolding you about this. It never occurred to me that there was another animal that could be responsible."

Aldo nodded his head. "It's okay," he said. "I know you were upset."

Even though his pets were no longer being accused of destroying his neighbor's lawn, Aldo offered to try and patch it up still one more time. Mrs. Crosby said she would call an exterminator to attend to the raccoon.

The word *exterminator* disturbed Aldo. He didn't want the raccoon killed. He wished he could make it into a pet, but raccoons were on the illegal list on his bulletin board.

After Aldo and DeDe took the dogs outside for a morning run, they sat down to a breakfast of French toast made by Karen. Aldo was extra careful with the bottle of syrup this morning.

When they finished eating, they went to work on the lawn. While they were on their hands and knees attempting to replace the clumps of grass that the raccoon had pulled up, a small van appeared in front of the house and a man stepped out.

"I can see you had some company last night,"

the driver said to Mrs. Crosby, who had come outside now, too.

The lettering on the van said WILDLIFE REMOVAL: ANIMAL PESTS MAKE UNWELCOME GUESTS.

"Are you going to kill that raccoon?" asked Aldo anxiously. It seemed every day he had to worry about another type of animal being murdered.

The man shook his head. "No," he said. "We are a humane outfit. I'm going to set a trap, and when I catch your raccoon, I'll take him to a more rural area and set him free where he won't bother anyone."

Aldo smiled with relief.

The man went to the back of the van and took out a large cage. He walked about Aldo's yard and then went over to Mrs. Crosby's property. He set the cage down, half-hidden under a bush. Aldo and DeDe watched as he opened a jar of peanut butter. "This is a raccoon's favorite treat," the man said. He put a big lump of the peanut butter inside the cage. "For a raccoon, this is like a hot fudge sundae."

"I like butterscotch better," said Aldo, grinning.

"Then I'm going to give you money to buy a butterscotch sundae, and your friend can get one, too," said Mrs. Crosby. "I'm just so sorry I suspected your pets. And you've been so nice about fixing my lawn every day. I'm going to be sure and tell your parents how helpful you were," said the older woman. "When are they coming home?"

"My father is due back in a couple of days," said Aldo. "But I'm not sure about my mother. She wants to help take care of my grandfather. He had a big operation but he's going to be okay now."

"That's good," said Mrs. Crosby. "If only I could rent my house, everything would be just fine for all of us."

"How come you're renting it?" asked DeDe.

"I want to stay in Florida for six months to see if I like it," Mrs. Crosby explained. "But I don't want to sell my house yet. Perhaps I'll hate it away from here."

"Do they have raccoons in Florida?" asked Aldo. "It might be boring without them."

"They have alligators in the Everglades," offered DeDe. "I saw them on a show on TV."

"Thank goodness I'm not planning to move there," laughed Mrs. Crosby.

* * *

That evening around nine o'clock, while Aldo was in the midst of playing with Peanut and Butter in the living room, the telephone rang. Elaine (whose hair was beginning to look less green) was off at a movie with Scott. Karen had a job that evening baby-sitting. So it was Aldo who answered the phone. It was his father.

"How's California?" asked Aldo.

"Surprise," said his father. "I'm not in California. I'm in Florida with your mother. I managed to cut my trip short so I could join her here. Your grandfather is doing fine. But neither your mother nor I feel that your grandmother should have to take care of him on her own. So in a few days, as soon as the doctor says he is strong enough, we will all come back to Woodside together."

"All of you?" asked Aldo.

"Yep. We're going to have a full house," said Mr. Sossi. "Karen will have to move into Elaine's bedroom temporarily."

"Okay," said Aldo, wondering if Elaine and Karen would find this arrangement okay.

"There's something we have to discuss, Aldo,"

said Mr. Sossi. "I think we're going to have a problem with the puppies."

"What kind of a problem?" asked Aldo nervously.

"There just is too much commotion with two dogs underfoot. We're going to have to find another home for one of them."

"Oh, Dad. I couldn't do that," said Aldo. "This is home—for both of them. And they hardly have any accidents these days. I just can't give one away. Please. Can't I keep them both?"

"Well. Don't worry about it now," said Mr. Sossi. "The important thing is that your grandfather is coming along fine." He paused for a moment. "Let me speak with your sisters," he suggested.

"They aren't here now," said Aldo. "Just me and Peanut and Butter. Would you like to talk to one of them?" He didn't wait for an answer. He put the phone down and made a grab for the nearest dog. It was Butter, and she was right at his feet chewing on the laces of his sneakers.

Aldo picked up the receiver and put it near the dog's mouth. Amazingly, Butter barked into the phone. He hadn't taught the dogs to sit or stay or roll over or any of those other tricks he had read about. But Butter knew how to talk on the telephone. He could hardly wait to finish speaking with his father so he could call DeDe and tell her about that, too. Butter could talk to her!

Aldo's mother got on the phone. "We'll be home in just a few days," she said. "Is everything going all right?"

"Everything's fine here," said Aldo. It was too complicated to tell his mother everything on the telephone—the news about Elaine's hair or the lobsters or the raccoon in Mrs. Crosby's yard. He'd save all that for when his parents were home again.

"Give my love to Elaine and Karen. I'll speak with them tomorrow," said Mrs. Sossi. She made a funny sound into the phone. Aldo knew it was a kiss. Since no one was around except Peanut and Butter, he sent her a kiss via the phone wires to Florida, too.

"Guess what?" he said to his puppies. "You're going to meet my grandparents in a few days." Then he remembered that one of them might have to go.

He just had to figure out a way to convince his parents that two puppies were not too many.

Aldo sat down on the sofa. He felt something damp. Too late, he realized that he had been so busy playing and speaking on the phone he had missed taking the dogs for their evening walk. He went to get the leashes. As he walked across the room, he noticed that it was in a terrible mess. Papers and books on the floor; shoes, socks, and dishes were everywhere. If his parents walked in right now, they would be in a state of shock. A big cleanup was in order, and fast.

Undoing the Mess

When Karen returned home from baby-sitting at eleven o'clock, she found Aldo on his hands and knees trying to get a big stain out of the living room carpet. And when Elaine came home from the movies at eleven-thirty, she found both Aldo and Karen on their hands and knees wiping the chair legs with damp sponges.

"What's going on?" asked Elaine.

"Mom and Dad are coming home in a few days and they're bringing Grandma and Grandpa with them," said Aldo.

"And everything in this house is sticky," said Karen.

Elaine slid her hand across the coffee table, and then she felt the sofa. "Yuck. How did everything get so sticky?" she asked.

"I don't know," said Karen.

Aldo knew. But he wasn't going to admit it. When Butter had the pancake syrup all over her, she got it all over the house, too. He wondered if they would ever be able to get things back to normal.

"It's too late to clean now," said Elaine. "Let's go to bed. Tomorrow we'll do something about all this. I think the carpet needs to be shampooed," she added, looking at the stain that Aldo had been unsuccessful in removing.

"I didn't know that carpets had shampoos," marveled Aldo as he stood up.

"Live and learn," called Elaine as she went up to her bedroom. Aldo didn't tell her that when their grandparents arrived, she would have to share the room with Karen. She'd have to live and learn, he decided.

In the morning, the three junior members of the

Sossi family took a good look around the house. It was not just the living room that was a mess. In the kitchen, almost every dish the family owned was in the sink or on the counter waiting to be washed. Karen loved to cook, but she didn't see why she should be expected to wash up the dishes, too. And Elaine's philosophy was that as long as there were still clean dishes in the cupboard, why worry about the dirty ones?

The dining room was even stickier than the living room. After all, that's where the bottle of syrup had actually spilled. Peanut and Butter ran about, close to Aldo's heels, as he surveyed the house. There was no avoiding the blame. The two dogs had done more than their share to make a once neat and pleasant home into one huge mess. But Aldo knew he couldn't blame them. When his mother was home, the dogs were always kept in the kitchen area. He had thought it wouldn't do any harm to let them have some freedom. He had been a hundred percent wrong about that.

"We've got to get everything back in order before Mom and Dad get here," said Karen. "Otherwise,

Mom will say she was right that she shouldn't have left us on our own."

"If Grandpa walked in here and saw the place the way it is now, he'd probably have a relapse. He'd fall right down on the rug," said Aldo.

"And what's more, the rug is so sticky he'd never get up again," said Elaine. "We better get to work fast."

"I don't see how Grandma and Grandpa can stay here," said Karen. "This house isn't big enough for so many people." She began to count. "There's five of us, and Grandma and Grandpa will make two more—that's seven. And then there's Peabody and Peanut and Butter. There just isn't enough room."

Aldo didn't tell her that she was going to have to move into Elaine's bedroom during the forth-coming extended visit of their grandparents. But he did say, "Dad says I might have to give up one of the puppies."

"Oh, Aldo. He couldn't be so mean."

Aldo bit his lip and swallowed hard. He didn't want to start thinking about surrendering one of the dogs. It would make him cry. Instead, he went into the bathroom and located the bottle of shampoo in the medicine cabinet. He decided he would start with the living room rug. Karen and Elaine remained in the kitchen. They were going to tackle the dishes.

Aldo poured some shampoo on the rug and began to rub it into the fabric with his fingers. Butter stuck her nose in the lather, but for once something did not appeal to her taste buds. She ran away.

After a few minutes of working the shampoo into the rug, Aldo wondered how he would rinse the soap out of the rug.

"I need a glass of water," he announced to his sisters as he entered the kitchen.

"We just washed all the glasses," complained Karen. "I don't want them getting dirty again."

"Do we have to eat with our fingers so we don't dirty the forks and spoons from now on, too?" asked Aldo. "Besides, I need the water to rinse the shampoo out of the rug."

"What shampoo?" asked Elaine.

"The shampoo I used to wash the rug. You said last night that it needed a shampoo."

"Don't you know anything?" asked Elaine. "You don't use *people* shampoo on a rug."

"I did," said Aldo.

"How is this going to dry out?" asked Elaine as she inspected Aldo's handiwork. "You got the rug soaking wet."

Aldo thought for a moment and ran up the stairs. "I can use this," he said, returning to the living room holding Elaine's portable hair dryer. "You always use it after a shampoo."

He plugged the dryer into the nearest outlet and aimed it at the wet carpet.

"It's going to take forever. We only have a couple of days. But look, the stain is gone. The shampoo really worked," said Aldo proudly.

"Why don't you go into business?" said Elaine sarcastically.

"What about the sofa?" asked Karen. "If you get that wet, it will never dry."

"I think we'll have to get a professional cleaning service to help us out," said Elaine.

"That will cost a fortune," complained Karen.

"We can do it ourselves," said Aldo. "Look, the rug is getting drier already."

Karen and Elaine rubbed their fingers on the portion of the rug where Aldo had been aiming the dryer.

It was tedious work. But Aldo knew that he had to do it. If everything was in order when his parents came home, maybe they would let him keep both dogs, after all. So when Aldo got tired of holding the dryer, he took a break and found another chore to do instead. He picked up all the books and magazines that were lying around. He sorted out the shoes and sneakers and put them all away.

Karen got out the furniture polish and was using it on all the wooden pieces. Soon the downstairs of the Sossi house had a lemon smell from the polish.

Elaine took out the vacuum cleaner and got into every corner. "Look at this," she shrieked above the sound of the motor. *This* was a chewed-up sock.

"What was a sock doing on the living room floor?" shouted Karen.

"It won't happen again," Aldo promised above the din of the vacuum. He had locked Peanut and Butter into the kitchen.

By lunchtime, the downstairs was looking pretty good. Of course, they still had to attend to the

upstairs. None of the beds had been made all week. And because Peanut and Butter had gotten upstairs, there were plenty of traces of their rampage on the second floor, just as there had been on the first.

Although Karen rarely was too tired to cook, today she didn't have any energy to fix lunch. "Besides, I don't want to dirty a single dish or risk spilling anything on the floor," she said. "It's hard work doing all this cleaning. Let's go buy a pizza."

Aldo got the leashes to walk the dogs while his sisters caught their breaths and combed their hair. (Elaine's hair had a green cast only in direct sunlight. Sometimes you couldn't notice it at all.)

As Aldo walked past Mrs. Crosby's house, both puppies began barking furiously. They pulled Aldo over to Mrs. Crosby's yard and in the direction of the bush where the cage had been hidden the day before. There was a noise coming from the cage. The raccoon had been caught. For a moment, Aldo stood looking at the raccoon in fascination as the puppies barked furiously at the caged animal.

The poor raccoon was frightened and furious at the same time. His strong teeth bit at the heavy bars of the cage. Even though this was the villain who was responsible for all the hours Aldo had spent working on Mrs. Crosby's lawn, he felt sorry for the creature. Poor thing. No amount of delicious peanut butter could be worth the terror the animal was experiencing now.

Aldo pulled Peanut and Butter away and took them for their walk. When the dogs were returned to the Sossi kitchen, Aldo, Karen, and Elaine set out for their pizza lunch.

"Look," Aldo said to his sisters. "The raccoon has been captured."

He took them over to the cage. As they stood gaping at the raccoon, the man from Wildlife Removal drove up in his van. He had come to take the cage and its occupant away.

"Where are you taking him?" Aldo asked. He watched as the man put on very heavy gloves to protect his hands from the raccoon's teeth.

"There's a wildlife preserve about thirty miles from here," the man said. "There's where I take all the raccoons I catch. Yesterday I brought a mama squirrel and a nest of babies that I removed from someone's chimney there, too."

Aldo hoped the wildlife preserve was filled with

loads of grubs for the raccoon to eat. He wanted the animal to be happy in his new home.

"Did you find someone to rent your house yet?" Aldo asked Mrs. Crosby, who had come outside to watch the raccoon's departure.

"No," said their neighbor. "It doesn't seem as if anyone is interested in living in Woodside. Or at least, they're not interested in living in my house." She sighed.

"Don't worry," said Aldo. "Someone will rent your place yet. Especially since now your lawn isn't going to be dug up every night."

"What's that all about?" asked Karen as they walked down the street.

"Mrs. Crosby is trying to rent her house," said Aldo.

No sooner had he said those words than Aldo was struck with an idea. Maybe, just maybe, he had a solution to everyone's problem.

CHAPTER 10

Mrs. Crosby Rents Her House

By the afternoon of the day when Mr. and Mrs. Sossi were expected home again, the inside of their house on Hillside Lane had taken on a wonderful glow. Every piece of furniture was polished and shining. The rugs were free of stains; the upholstery was no longer sticky. Even the curtains had been taken down and washed and ironed.

Elaine had made bouquets of fresh flowers and placed them around the house. Everything looked as if it was waiting for a photographer from *House Beautiful* to come and take pictures for a feature article in the next issue of the magazine.

In addition to the attractive appearance of all the rooms, there was a wonderful aroma coming from the house. After a day and a half of not wanting to get any of the dishes soiled, Karen had begun to cook again. She had done it on the condition that Aldo and Elaine immediately wash any dirty dishes that accumulated in the sink. Now there was a turkey roasting in the oven and two blueberry pies cooling on the kitchen counter.

"It smells just like Thanksgiving in here," said Aldo, coming to get Peanut and Butter from the kitchen, where they were once again strictly enclosed.

"We have a lot to be thankful for," said Karen. "Grandpa is getting better."

"I'm thankful that you can hardly see the green in my hair," said Elaine.

Aldo attached the leashes to the dogs. "I'll watch for the taxi," he said.

Mr. and Mrs. Sossi and Aldo's grandparents were expected at any time now. At first, Elaine had tried to arrange that Mrs. Lorin would drive them all to the airport so that they could greet all the adults when they emerged from their plane. But in the end, it was decided to remain at the house and have a WEL-COME HOME banner attached to the front door instead.

Aldo walked past Mrs. Crosby's house. Mrs. Crosby was sitting on a lawn chair in front of her house. She waved to Aldo as he passed. "Next week at this time, I'll be sitting on a beach chair," she called to him.

Mrs. Crosby was finally going to Florida. It had taken four telephone calls to make all the arrangements. "You would make a fine real estate agent," Mrs. Crosby had told Aldo. After all, it was Aldo who had come up with the plan about Mrs. Crosby's house. Mrs. Crosby wanted to go to Florida. Aldo's grandparents, who lived in Florida, were going to spend some time in Woodside. It made good sense that they temporarily exchange homes.

Aldo had phoned his father. His father had spoken to his mother. His mother had spoken to her mother. Aldo's parents had spoken to Mrs. Crosby. Tonight and tomorrow evening, Aldo's grandparents would sleep in Karen's room. That was to give Mrs. Crosby time to finish packing and to give her a chance to meet and speak with her tenants. Then she was going off to Florida, and Karen would have her bedroom back again when her grandparents moved next door. Everyone was very pleased with this arrangement. But no one was happier than Aldo. There was no more talk these days of giving away one of his puppies.

A taxi was coming down the street. Aldo pulled in the leashes so that the dogs knew he wanted to stand still. He watched as the taxi slowed down and then came to a halt in front of his house. "Come on," he yelled to the dogs. "They're here!" He ran to the car, pulling the dogs along with him.

Aldo watched as his father jumped out of the front seat of the taxi and then helped his grandfather out of the back. Aldo's grandfather looked older and more frail than Aldo remembered him. But his smile when he saw Aldo was the same. And when the old man was introduced to the newest family members, Peanut and Butter, the smile became broader still.

Both dogs jumped up at once to greet the visitor. "Down," commanded Aldo's grandfather. He spoke with authority. It was a tone of voice that Aldo had never heard before. And wonder of wonders, it was a voice that the two dogs immediately obeyed.

"These dogs need some training," Aldo's grandfather said.

"I'm trying," said Aldo. "But it isn't easy, and besides, they're still puppies."

"They're older than they were yesterday," said his grandfather. "I can see you need some help. It's a good thing that I'm here."

"Now, Paul. Don't exert yourself," said Aldo's grandmother to her husband in an anxious voice as she got out of the taxi.

She was prevented from further comment by Elaine and Karen, who had rushed outside to greet the arriving family members. There were hugs and kisses all around.

Aldo noticed that despite all the excitement, both Peanut and Butter remained sitting. They didn't jump and they didn't bark. That was not how they ordinarily would have reacted in such a situation.

"Look how the dogs obey you," Aldo said to his grandfather.

"Dogs want to obey," the old man said. "But they have to know you mean what you say." He

smiled at his grandson. "I've owned a few dogs in my day. I know all about them and I'll teach you as well as them."

"Super!" said Aldo.

That evening the five Sossis and the two grandparents ate the turkey dinner that Karen had prepared. (Aldo didn't eat the turkey, but he ate everything else that Karen had cooked.)

"You can really feel proud of these children," said Aldo's grandmother, turning to Mrs. Sossi. "Not every family has three youngsters who can take care of themselves, keep a house in such good order, and make such a delicious meal, too."

Aldo looked at his sisters. They grinned at each other sheepishly. Imagine if their parents had walked in on them a few days ago! Elaine unconsciously ran her fingers through her hair. Aldo knew she was mighty relieved that no one had noticed the trace of green that was still there.

"Karen, this pie crust is as good as any I've ever eaten," complimented her grandmother.

"You should taste her dog biscuits," said Aldo. "I hear they are pretty good, too."

Elaine blushed. But neither Aldo nor Karen gave away that secret, either.

Aldo's grandparents were tired after their day of travel. So, shortly after dinner, they rose from the table to go up to Karen's bedroom. They had already met Mrs. Crosby and looked over her house.

Aldo took the dog leashes from their hook and attached them to his puppies' collars. "Time for your evening walk," he told them.

"Remember, you're the boss," said Aldo's grandfather.

Aldo grinned. "Right!" he said, standing tall and holding firmly to the leashes.

The rest of the summer was going to be a busy one, he thought. He wanted to learn all he could from his grandfather about dog training before he had to go back to school. Maybe after Peanut and Butter had mastered the basic skills, like sitting and staying, his grandfather could help teach them some advanced tricks, too. He wanted his dogs to know how to shake paws and to roll over and to catch a Frisbee.

He went out into the evening dusk. There was just a single light on in Mrs. Crosby's house. Even though she was nowhere in sight, Aldo smiled in his neighbor's direction. It was great that she was exchanging homes for the next few months with his grandparents. It was great, too, that his grandfather had recovered so well from his operation. And now it would be super to have them living so near. Everything was working out fine.

Aldo gave a tug to the puppies' leashes. They didn't know how close they had come to being parted. One of them almost had to go to a new home. It was a terrible possibility. But, thankfully, it had been avoided. "Come on, fellows. Let's get some exercise," Aldo called.

And Aldo Sossi, Peanut, and Butter ran down the length of Hillside Lane.